Afro Puffs Held High

Written by Frieda Millhouse-Jones
Illustrated by Miks Quinto

BOOKLOGIX
K I D S

BOOKLOGIX
KIDS

Alpharetta, GA

ISBN: 978-1-6653-0558-7 - Paperback
eISBN: 978-1-6653-0559-4 - ePub
eISBN: 978-1-6653-0560-0 - mobi

Library of Congress Control Number: 2022922175

1 2 0 7 2 2

∞ This paper meets the requirements of ANSI/NISO Z39.48-1992 (Permanence of Paper)

Illustrated by Miks Quinto

To my girls, Morgan, Olivia and Callan,
Your bravery inspires me every day.

To my husband, Terrance,
Your unwavering love gives me wings.

Thank you all for supporting me in this journey.

Frieda

I was not going to school that day. As I ate my breakfast, I looked out the window and saw my friends getting onto the bus as usual.

"Livi Lou, it's time to go," said Mom.

I threw away my trash and left. Mom turned out the lights and locked the door for the last time.

I helped Dad put the last boxes into the car and waved goodbye to our house. The curtains were all gone, and the house looked lonely.

We drove away.

I clutched Jerry the Giraffe tightly to my chest.
Gusts of wind whispered into the back seat, swirling
through my afro puffs and cooling my tears.

We drove past the school where I'd started second grade.
All my classmates were playing hide and seek.

The playground was a beautiful mix of all the colors.

I waved at my friends, but no one saw me. We drove all day and into the night.

When we got to our new house, it was **snowing!** I had never seen snow before.

The next day, I dressed in my favorite navy blue sweater dress. My mom did my hair that morning with two large fluffy afro puffs. She tied two bright red ribbons around my hair.

Then Mom walked with me to the main door of my new school.

I could feel the butterflies in my stomach. I hoped my new teacher would be nice. Would I be able to make new friends? Would the playground be as fun as the one at my old school?

When I walked into my classroom, everyone stopped and stared.

No one looked like me. I didn't like it at all.

I was quiet all that morning.
Then the bell rang for recess. All the kids grabbed their boots
and coats and mittens and hats and rushed outside.
I was the last one out to the playground.
I had to play alone.

Finally, it was time to go home. I got off the school bus, ran inside, and slammed the door.

"My new school is awful," I shrieked.
I fell onto the couch, hugged my dog, and began to sob.

"I don't feel like I belong there at all. I want to go back to my old school!"

Mom and Dad both put their arms
around me and squeezed tight. "It's just
the first day, my darling Livi Lou,"
said Mom. "Things will get better," said Dad.
"Please, just give it more time."

More days passed by. Things did not get any better. One day, a mean girl named Tabitha teased me on the playground.

She stuck her tongue out and made fun of my hair. I wanted to run and hide. I felt smaller and smaller. I didn't know what to do.

I cried myself to sleep that night.

But then, I had a wonderful dream:
My afro puffs lit up. They floated me up into
the air like a balloon. I was flying high.
Even better, I could fly back in time!

In my dream, my magic puffs took me to a school in New Orleans, Louisiana.

I saw a small girl named Ruby Bridges. She was only six years old. The people in the crowd were **yelling** mean things at her as she walked up the school steps. The people were mad that she was the first Black child to attend this all-white school.

She had to be escorted by police. She was very brave.

Next, I flew over to Greensboro, North Carolina. I could see four Black college students sitting at a lunch counter.

They wanted to be able to eat at the same counter as whites. They sat as people **yelled** and **threw** things at them. They sat unmoved and did not fight back. The Greensboro Four stayed peaceful even though they were scared.

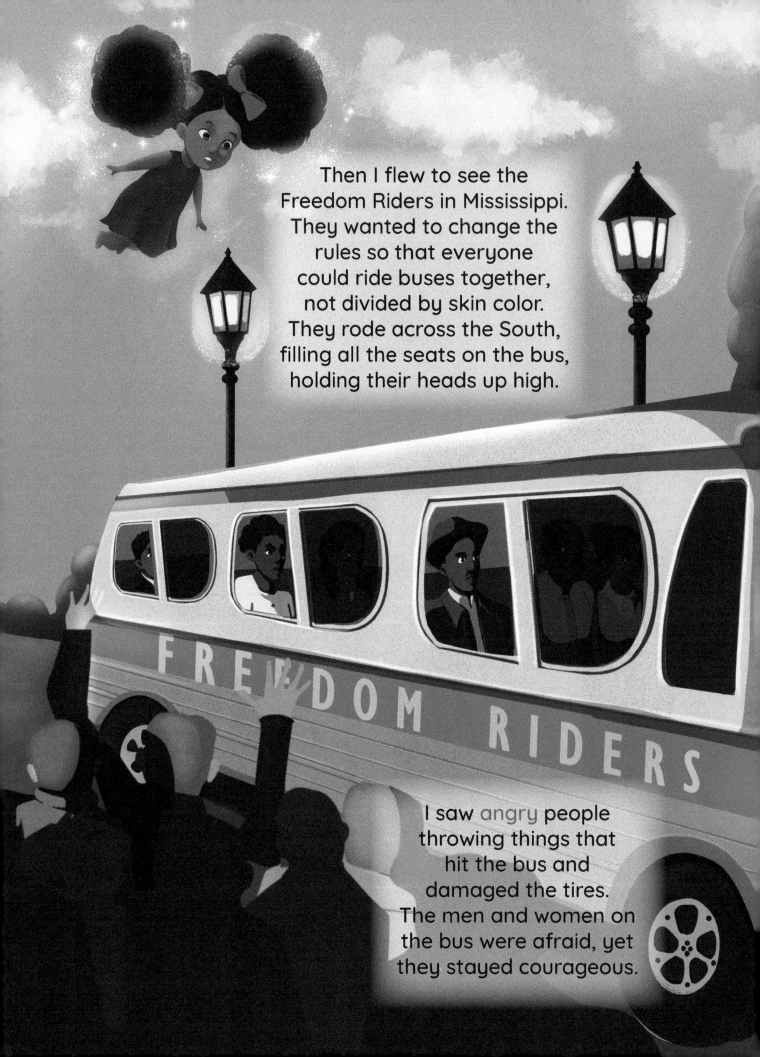

Then I flew to see the Freedom Riders in Mississippi. They wanted to change the rules so that everyone could ride buses together, not divided by skin color. They rode across the South, filling all the seats on the bus, holding their heads up high.

I saw angry people throwing things that hit the bus and damaged the tires. The men and women on the bus were afraid, yet they stayed courageous.

For my last stop, I flew over to see the Children's Crusade of 1963. Young children marched peacefully. They walked down the streets of Birmingham, Alabama.

They continued to march even though the police sprayed them with powerful water hoses and attacked them with dogs.

Some children were even sent to jail. They wanted the world to see that it was unfair to have laws separating whites and Blacks.

I woke up from my dream. I felt stronger, more confident.
I had learned something from that dream.
*The strength of those who came before me
lives inside of me.*

With my new understanding, I jumped out of bed, brushed my teeth, and got dressed. I rode the bus with my head held high like the Freedom Riders.

I walked up to the school unafraid like Ruby Bridges.
I marched down the hall like the children in the Crusade.
I took my seat like the Greensboro Four. I raised my hand.
I can be strong, even when I'm scared.

When I got home,
I gently patted my
magical afro puffs,
thankful.

I could not help but smile.
I am living my ancestors'
dreams. I can do anything
because I have their strength
inside of me.

The End

About the Author

Frieda Millhouse-Jones M. D. is a practicing primary care physician in Atlanta, GA. She developed a love of reading at a very young age. One of her favorite memories is of getting her book of the month by mail and excitedly reading it the same day. She wants to share the same passion for reading with young people across the globe. She is fiercely dedicated to empowering young girls to overcome adversity by using her personal life experiences. Her previous works and advocacy seek to raise awareness surrounding issues of perfectionism, racism, and mental health. She enjoys naps, travel and yoga. She currently lives with her husband, two daughters and two very mischievous dogs.

CPSIA information can be obtained
at www.ICGtesting.com
Printed in the USA
LVHW071441030123
736350LV00027B/342